P9-DMX-499

William Tell

William Tell

LEONARD EVERETT FISHER

DISCARDED
from
New Hanover County Public Library

FARRAR, STRAUS AND GIROUX · NEW YORK

For my granddaughter, Lauren Nicole, with love

Copyright © 1996 by Leonard Everett Fisher
All rights reserved. Published simultaneously in Canada by HarperCollins*CanadaLtd*.
Color separations by Hong Kong Scanner Arts. Printed in the United States of America
by Berryville Graphics. Designed by Filomena Tuosto. First edition, 1996

Library of Congress Cataloging-in-Publication Data
Fisher, Leonard Everett.
William Tell / Leonard Everett Fisher. — 1st ed.
p.   cm.
1. Tell, Wilhelm—Legends. [1. Tell, Wilhelm—Legends. 2. Folklore—Switzerland.]
I. Title. PZ8.1.F545Wl 1996 398.—dc20 [398.2'0949402] 95-13861 CIP AC

ʰigh above Gessler Square, the Town Hall bell clanged furiously. It echoed through the mountains like a dozen bells ringing at once. People rushed to the square.

"A proclamation!" cried the herald as he unrolled a long parchment.

"Know ye by all those present that, from noon of this day forward, all citizens, including children ten years and older, must kneel before the hat of the royal governor, Herr Gessler. The hat will be mounted atop a pole in Gessler Square in the Town of Altdorf in the Canton of Uri under the jurisdiction of King Albert I of the House of Hapsburg. Failure to kneel will result in swift and severe punishment.

"Signed and sealed this First Day of July in the Year of Our Lord 1307."

"He is cruel, that Hermann Gessler," William Tell growled to his young son, Jemmy. "A tyrant if ever there was one."

Tell, a famous hunter and marksman, lived with his family in nearby Bürglen. He and Jemmy were passing through Altdorf on their way to the forest when they heard the proclamation.

"If I had my way," a woman whispered, "it would be Herr Gessler at the end of the royal pole, not his hat."

"Ssssh," someone in the crowd warned. "Just kneel and be still."

No one spoke too loudly about anything in Altdorf, Bürglen, or any other town in Uri. Herr Gessler's spies were everywhere. A sneeze at the wrong time could bring ten days in jail.

A little before noon, a small parade of officials and soldiers led by Herr Gessler left Altdorf's Town Hall. They marched to the center of the square. There they watched the raising of a pole with Gessler's hat on top.

"Careful! Careful, you louts!" snapped Herr Gessler as the pole was slowly placed upright. "You will pay dearly if my hat falls to the ground."

As the Town Hall clock began to strike noon, Herr Gessler took his seat next to the pole. The first passerby knelt before his hat and hurried off.

"Aha," he said. "Very good. Very good, indeed."

People passed this way and that, knelt, then left the square as quickly as they could. None of them had the courage to look at Herr Gessler, whose scornful face was enough to frighten a farsighted deer.

But before the Town Hall clock had finished delivering its booming twelve strokes of noon, a young man with a pig to deliver rushed by and forgot to kneel.

"Arrest that lawbreaker!" screamed Gessler. "Arrest his pig, too!"

Soldiers swarmed all over the young man. They took away his pig and clapped him in chains as he begged for another chance.

"Never!" Herr Gessler shouted after him.

No sooner had the young man been dragged out of sight, howling for mercy, than a teenage boy, chased by his older sister, ran across the square.

"Come home this instant!" cried his sister.

"No!" replied the boy. And the two of them sailed past Herr Gessler like the wind. They, too, forgot to kneel.

"Seize those two!" Herr Gessler commanded.

The boy and his sister were chained and hauled away.

All day long, men, women, and children ten years and older rushed through Gessler Square. They knelt before Herr Gessler's hat—some of them three, four, or more times.

"This is mean and stupid," William Tell said to Jemmy as the two returned to the square. They were on their way home from the forest.

"Gessler may be the governor of Uri, but we are not his slaves and lackeys. I shall never kneel before him or his hat."

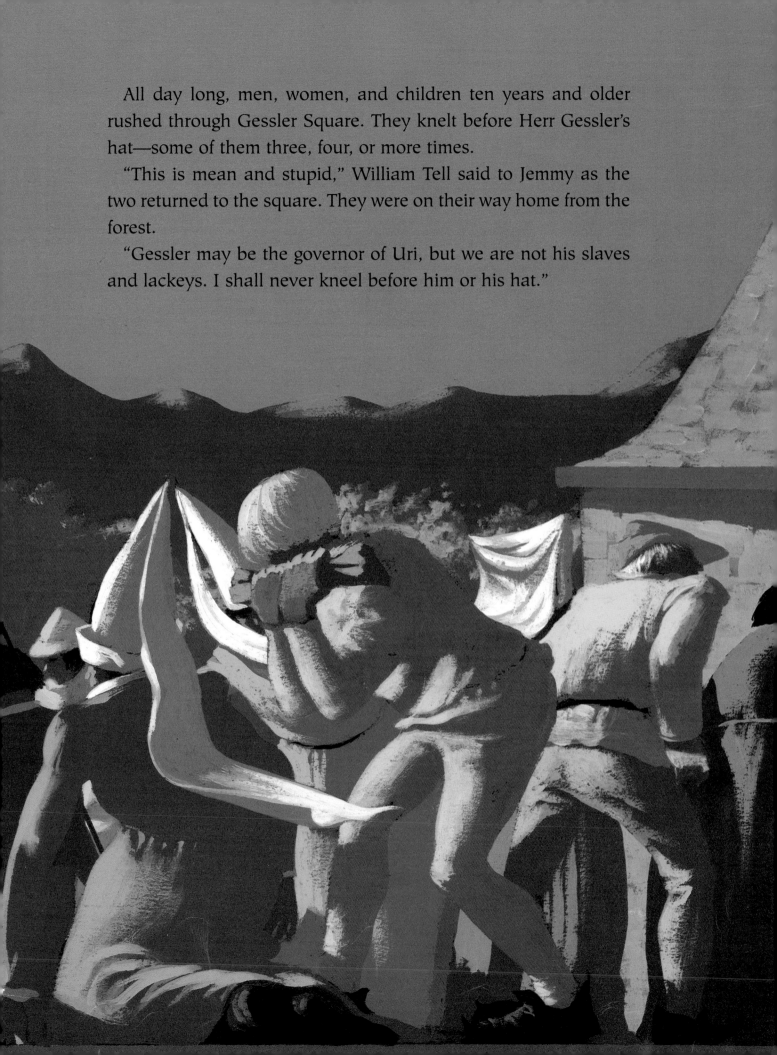

William Tell and Jemmy slowly walked past the pole. Herr Gessler was still in his chair, ready to pounce on anyone who did not kneel. "You two there, William Tell, Jemmy Tell!" he cried. "How dare you walk by my hat and not kneel? You know the law! Kneel, I say!"

"Kneel, you say. Walk on, I say. Neither I nor my son shall kneel before the hat of a bully."

Herr Gessler shook with rage. No one moved. It was as if the square had suddenly filled with wide-eyed marble statues.

"Arrest them!" Herr Gessler roared. "Throw them into the dungeon! Flog them! Tear out their nails! No. Wait. I have a better idea.

"So you say I am a bully, Herr Tell? The law is the law. But I shall show you what a fair and decent man I am. For your disobedience and disrespect, I order you to shoot a single arrow through an apple placed on the head of your son. You shall be allowed only one shot at sixty paces. Should you pierce the apple, I shall set you free. Furthermore, no one need ever kneel before my hat again.

"However, should the arrow fail to hit the apple, your son will either perish at your hand or be freed by mine. But you, Herr Tell, shall go to prison, where you shall rot forever. And my new law shall remain on the books."

The crowd stirred.

William Tell looked at Jemmy. His heart pounded in his chest. What if he should miss?

He made up his mind to shoot wide of the mark and go to prison rather than risk harming his son. That way, Jemmy would live and go free. But was Gessler to be trusted, he wondered.

"You must do this, Father," Jemmy pleaded, "for all the people. I am not afraid. You are the best marksman in Uri."

William Tell took a moment to decide. "All right, Jemmy. I shall do it," he said.

A wicked grin covered Herr Gessler's face.

One of Gessler's soldiers positioned Jemmy against a wide tree. Another soldier placed a red apple on his head.

Sixty paces away, William Tell fitted his crossbow with an arrow. Hidden in his cloak was a second arrow.

The crowd moved back. Herr Gessler leaned forward in his chair.

William Tell took his time. He squinted down the path his arrow would take. He looked hard at the apple on Jemmy's head. He held the crossbow straight and steady in front of him and lined up the arrow with the center of the apple.

William Tell let the arrow fly.

23.

It tore the apple in two.

The crowd cheered. Jemmy smiled. Herr Gessler slumped in his chair.

As William Tell and his son bowed before the happy throng, the hidden arrow fell to the ground.

Herr Gessler bolted from his chair. "You were allowed only one shot, Herr Tell. For what purpose did you need another arrow?"

"This second arrow was for you, Herr Gessler. Had the first arrow harmed my son, I would have sent the second through your evil heart."

"Assassin!" cried Gessler. "Seize him. The law stands! The people shall kneel before my hat on the pole."

William Tell, wrapped in chains, was led away.

A week later, a chorus of bells clanged through the mountains. The people of Altdorf, Bürglen, and all the other towns of Uri were greeted with startling news. Hermann Gessler was dead!

William Tell had escaped his captors. Free of his chains, he had jumped from a storm-tossed boat heading for the prison on Lake Luzern. Gessler himself had led a troop of soldiers in search of him.

Armed with a bow and arrows made from a young tree in the forest, William Tell had waited for Herr Gessler. As the troop had galloped down a narrow trail, William Tell had sent a single arrow through Gessler's heart.

The people were rid of a cruel tyrant.

William Tell came home a hero forevermore.

NEW HANOVER COUNTY PUBLIC LIB.

3 4200 00406723 3

8/96

NEW HANOVER COUNTY PUBLIC LIBRARY
201 Chestnut Street
Wilmington, N.C. 28401

GAYLORD
S